END PIECES

End Pieces

Paul Bukovec

CONTENTS

1

SCENES, PORTRAITS, STORIES AND REFLECTIONS

1.   A Chance Encounter
"time passes by while we're not looking"
Phillip Roth

Hurriedly
on my way,
down the busy
mid-town street
I looked up
cocked
my head
and,
in the corner
of my eye,
caught
glimpse
of an older

man walking
rapidly
alongside me
with a startled
bemused look
staring back
through
hooded
crease rimmed eyes...
I was surprised
to realize
that hoary headed
startled
older man
was me.

2

MUSICAL CHAIRS

In her late
thirties
with her
clock
ticking
and her
heart
beating
fast, she
cast aside
higher
expectations
discarded
loftier
standards
and
fell onto
him in a
desperate
scramble
for the

last
musical chair
when
she thought
the song
was
about
to stop.

in his early
forties
he found
her bottom
arriving in
his lap
an unforeseen
and comforting
reward for
reluctantly
participating
in a game
he had
previously
felt
too shy
and
too ineptly
unsuccessful
to play

so he,
surprised
at her

enthusiasm,
and
she,
grateful
for his
startled
appreciation,
fumbled
matrimonially
forward,
quickly
hoping
for the best,
quietly
dreading
the worst...
and...

awkwardness,
frustration
and
disappointment
ensued
in unfairly
short order.

curdling
sourly
over the
longer
haul

and

they lived
happily
hardly
ever
after.

3

AMORES PERROS

my Mexican getaway
with a newish girlfriend:
began with promise.
and devolved intermittently
along the journey.
our quirks of personality.
differences of style, and
conflicting moods ensured
bumpy roads, poor connections.

occasional synchronic
moments were inevitably
followed by stretches
of cranky snits. pouts,
or dueling disappointments.

we were fast becoming
an affair to remember
badly, as the trip ground
grimly to an end, we
caught a cab at the dock

on our way to the airport.
pantomimed our fare
negotiation. threw bags into
the shabby vehicle. readied
ourselves for a sullen ride.

radio blaring, zooming
down dusty side streets.
sharp, squealing turns.
suddenly we're racing up
a wide stretch of open road.
just then a scraggly street dog
appears ahead, running
diagonally across the highway
desperate for the other side.
instantly the cabby guns
the engine. races forward.
veers sharply. floors it.
runs the hapless animal
down and over. abrupt
thump. trash in the road.

the surly assassin flashes
a lascivious, psychopathic grin
into the rearview mirror.
catches my eye. I scowl.
confused. outraged.
girlfriend emits a wail,
curls into a ball deep
into the seat against my side.
Instinctively, I pull her to me.
hold her tight. say whatever
soothing somethings I can

muster. she is gut punched
breath and words gone.
trembling. sobbing silently.

at the terminal the exchange
is numb. wordless: bile. snot.
disgust. diverted looks.
brutal replays looping back
on repeat. throbbing heads.
teary red eyes.
we slog through the airport.
slow motion. underwater.
lugubriously towing luggage.
sharing secrets of private violation.
closer now than any moment
of our trip. viscerally connected.
empathically present. aware
to each other as not before.
comrades in trauma. we
ride that connection home.
and for a while forward...

in temporary reprieve from
our inevitable parting.

4

MOONLIT CRYSTALLINE HAIL

had fallen upon
the hyper-chilled
melt off,
and frozen fog
had descended
before dawn
to coat the walkways
with treacherous
black and white ice

undaunted
the older man
boldly ventured out
for his morning walk
stepping carefully
on the previous week's
shoveled snow
along the edges
of the sidewalks

to snag traction
and remain upright.

cars crawled in
low gear and drivers
clutched their wheels
with desperate
determination.

down the first hill
a steam shrouded
panel truck stood
astride the front garden
of a hapless neighbor
and two befuddled young men
laid branches and chains
behind spinning wheels.

the older man skated and
hop scotched/skidded on
beyond the marooned
van and slid round
the corner proudly
to a sunny straightaway
set his gyroscope and
centered the gravity
of his balancing act
well-enough to skate
over the glossy spots
and crunch down
onto the snowy strips
to reach the end of
that long block unscathed

and upright,
exuberantly agile.

crossing the well salted
main road was a cinch.
the older man bounded
to the opposite side
strutting proudly
while catching glimpse
of a sweet concerned face
of an older woman
in an SUV at the light.

he marched
forward, smiling
in jaunty recognition
of the gray headed lady,
his gaze lingering a moment
too long, as his foot fell fully
and firmly on to the handicap
cutout in the opposite curb.
suddenly he shot
(half-piping) up
catapulting
sideways, airborne.
his body,
as if remembering
ancient drills
his mind had
long since forgot
twisted, tucked
and curled
all the way over

almost in a ball
(he was
momentarily
impressed!)
before his elbow
painfully broke his fall
and his back rounded,
rolling him over hard
onto rudely
insulted knees.

the older woman rolled
down her window.
asked if he was all right.

the older man
flustered,
red of face
knelt upright
extended a thumb,

and lied.

said he was just fine.

5

JOSEPH (IF GOD SPARES HIM)

leather skin. mahogany
with cinnamon highlights.
years of hangin and workin
outside. deep crevices.
a face that smiled a lot
more back in the day, but
still can crack a broad one.

not a stylin man.
threadbare thrift store
rags for work; a few nice shirts;
a couple of pairs of better pants
he kept folded away
for special occasions. or
when he paid Ms. Dorothy
a visit once in a blue.

had a furnished room.
boarding house round
the corner from where

he came up in the fifties
and sixties. on-going-ly
amazed at still being alive,
having seen so many taken
and fallen along the way:

"do believe god spared me."

cold stone survivor. shoulda/
coulda/woulda been a casualty
of the streets. made it through
waves of crime, disease and
drug wars by the skin
of his dwindling teeth.
truth be told, Jo did
have natural and
uncanny street smarts.
a weird knack for getting
along. avoiding trouble.
keeping his head up or down,
depending what shit
happened on any given day.

inconsistent reports as to
his exact age. averaged out
to somewhere in his early
seventies. only child. scuffling
housekeeper church lady mom.
Jo left school to attend
a shoe store near Market,
where he spent time
gainfully stocking shelves,
sweeping up, breaking down

boxes, and running errands.

paid him out of petty cash.
ponied up a share to mama,
put a bit aside,
like she advised.
got "necessities"
at the candy counter.

Jo was agreeable. maybe
a touch on the simple side.
cept for that talent to smell
trouble from blocks away.
got recruited by a crew
that ran heroin out back
of a boarded-up house.
filled in as a lookout
on weekends. graduated
to runner. wound up
with a random bag
of product in a crazy frantic
police sweep. thought
to hawk it for the extra
cash. too scared.
dibbed and dabbed till
it was gone. left him
wanting bigger tastes.
before long Jo was riding
rocking horse round
the hood. lookin dusky,
dried out. on the nod.
mom wailed to see him
that way. lost to the streets.

became a lookout for break-ins
and burglaries. fed the beast.
slept in flop houses. got into
chronic ass backwards trying
to switch up on his high.
soon drifted into angel dust.
full frontal numb-na-tude.
could not tell one craving
from the other. nightmare
24/7. senses blunted.
street smarts stupefied.
useless for the game.
drifting on the job,
caught a burglary case
red handed.

remanded for treatment.
Salvation Army Shelter.
Roxborough. three squares
and a cot. three meetings
a day. old head sponsor.
bible. couple of almost
buddies. The Program.
return to jesus. gauzy haze.
horse- tranquilized slo-mo
brain still foggy, firing
behind the beat.
Jo Jo still a simple earnest
soul. still with the will to work.
NA lifer suggests window
washing: honest trade: low
overhead, avenues full

of potential customers.

not so burned out he can't
hustle, JoJo gathers pails,
rags, a squeegee. prowls
the Market. gets some regulars.
mom welcomes him back,
but he just can't go. she
blesses him anyway.
tells him she loves him every
day till the day she dies:
"god spared you," she says.
it becomes his raison d'être
AND his cautionary warning

ever after. setting up a plan
or simply making a date
to show up to do a job,
he'd finish with a humble
head bow, hold his worn cap
in his hands; offer his standby
caveat: "If god spares me".

6

BASIC TRAINING

daily we sat endlessly wary
in anxious agonized silence:
large circle. trainees and staff.
awaiting initiations, rituals.
gauntlets. trials by fire.

a group psychotherapy training
program. the doc in charge
possessing a unique blend
of scary brilliance, paranoid
rigidity, and the observing ego
of a Captain Queeg. lion-maned,
huge headed, surprisingly small
of body for a man of such
presence. chain smoking Pall Malls.
a Svengalian grinding axes.
mouthing reductionist axioms.
poker faced. penetrating eyes.
tiny dramatic flourishes: fingers
caressing cigarette pack cellophane.

leveraging constructed authority.

manipulating power, position,
and status. making and proving
points. unflappably cocksure. often
wrong. which we'd later come
to understand. everything intense.
provocations; random jabs; painful
revelations; artificially fabricated
confrontations, emotional outbursts...
learning by doing. and by being done.

heady times. total immersion. we
were consumed in the processes
of deep analysis of superficial
interaction. insights plumbed,
communications dissected,
personalities autopsied. before,
during and after work.
the immersion continued
all hours. we ate and slept
psychology. sub-grouped
and hung out obsessively
exploring one-another's navels.
innies or outies. closer to mom
or closer to dad. dependent
or counter-dependent. in or out
of the leader's favor. the best
and worst of times. exhilarating
and frightening allatonce together.

we were, at the very least, opened
to processing and being processed.
exposed to functioning under pressure.
taught some solid group dynamics.

at worst, we were dangled
over the edge of inappropriate
boundaries: in a schmergle
of privacy, work ethics, and
decorum, in daily transgression
of authority's limits: coerced
into that gray blur where training
stops and psycho-therapy begins.

most of us survived despite
the violations, conspiratorial
theories and cult-like practice
of the man in charge. most
acquired higher degrees,
advanced training, experienced
other mentors. most became more
expert, effective, flexible
professionals than the director
ever was. both because and
in spite of the ordeals endured.

most were unaware that the director
died prematurely. disgraced and
exiled in a drunken fall in his
own home, sustaining a fatal
injury his leonine head. his demise
failing to be noticed the obituary
sections of the local newspapers.

7

NEW NORMAL

up in the night
requires care.
pause for balance.
hand hold
at the dresser's edge.
steadying the legs.
waiting for feeling
in the feet.
knees to
unbuckle.

a few
faltering steps
to the toilet.
a hand on door jamb.
wobbliness
gives way
to the perpendicular.
to gratitude
for that droning
unhurried flow.

easy return
to disheveled
blankets.
twisted sheets.
pillows strewn.
crash test dummies.
my bedside car wreck.
I nestle
in again. belly
breathing, blanking
the mind, twisting,
nestling, contorting
to find that cozy
spot to fall off
the edge
of awareness.
again.

morning's wake
not quite
a reboot
of the mid-night
stumble bumble,
but close.

another pee.
hair strokes.
search for
ponytail tie.
phone,
slippers,
glasses:

the descent:
traumatized
learning
commands
one hand on the rail.
even as
the body comes alive,
the knees take time
to remember
the complexities
of down
the stairs.

direct
to the cappuccino
maker.
olfactory rituals:
ablutions.
loadings.
twistings.
swooshings.
foam frothing.
aromas rousing
remnants of lethargy.
cinnamon flavored
dark foam gathers
at the back
of the throat
seeping dark
bittersweet energy
slowly down my gullet.

the grip on the cereal

container,
like the banister
before, must be
purposeful, measured,
conscious, careful.

while old bones
and joints
awaken
gradually
to some
generous fraction
of their former
selves, they stay
a bit less in touch.
have less of
a handle on things
that can spill
into a disastrous
morning.

new territories
come with
new realities.

8

THE HUG

He was leaving
because he couldn't stay
after dropping in
to pleasantly surprise her
for a few moments
of conversation and croissants,
and the sight of her
rumpled round the house look,
the tantalizing tip
of her upper lip,
and the captivating,
totally endearing way
her mouth puckered
when she exhaled
the word chestnut.

So he stood at the door
lingering longer than he should,
arms encircling her slightly stiff back,
his chest luxuriating
in the schmear
of her comforting breasts,

as one hand
drifted slowly south
respectfully yearning
to stay and play,
but just pulling her closer,
suggesting the wish for more.

She cupped
the sides of his face
with her hands;
gently whispered:
"sweet man.".

Face flushed, neck tingling
he clenched her to him,
stunned and breathless
in sudden return for a few
quickened beats
to that delighted place
from far ago where
he had always,
without realizing,
longed to return.

9

A ONCE AND FORMER FRIEND

we were in our
mid-twenties.
vastly different
backgrounds.
thrown together
in a mental hospital
training program.

he, from an upper
middle class
suburban home;
I, from an urban,
north jersey, fourth
floor walk-up.

he went to Yale.
I, to a small, Catholic
college in New York.

he was privileged

and Jewish.
bit of a prince.
part rich-boy-wanna-be.
part seventies-boho-hippie.
educated. smart.
slacker. gentleman's
C-Student.

I wore my class
background
as an epaulet.
my politics
like armor.
flashed my
history-of-ideas
education, years
in drama and debate
and time abroad
teaching in Africa
whenever possible
during team meetings
and encounter groups.
hid my fears beneath
bravura challenges
to the leadership.

I could tell he admired
my ballsiness.
I liked his humor
and charm.

still recall
how he'd pause

to notice afternoon
light. or a certain shade
of blue on the horizon;
how he'd go on about
Brutalism or Morgan horses.
how he'd steal food
from his wife's plate
in restaurants.

recall his stubbornly
narrow taste in music,
yet his surprising
passion for Steely Dan.
Bonnie Raitt and Lou Reed.

his hatred of football.

still wince.
blink my mind's eye.
shake my head
ruefully
whenever intruded upon
by the recollection
of that time he got
arrested for shoplifting
a trivial tchotchke
in a nearby aquarium
store. or when the albino
gay waiter at Lickety Split
ran after him
out onto South Street
for not tipping.
or the embarrassing

revelations
of duplicitous
dishonesties
that rocked our circle
during his divorce.

we moved
away
and from
each other.
first gradually.
then all at once.

nowadays
he barely
comes to mind

but I still
think of him
in certain
afternoon light
or facing a poured
concrete office building
or passing
a horse farm.

or wondering
if my wife
is going to finish
that tid-bit
on her plate.

10

TWO KINDS OF PEOPLE IN THE WORLD?

years ago, still early
in my career, I was
tasked with evaluating
a very old black man.

neatly dressed, respectfully
polite. he presented himself
straightforwardly. direct.
answered questions openly.

had seen a great deal.
lived been through much.
witnessed riots. street wars,
plagues, and pestilence.

educated by hard work
and hard knocks.
trials and tribulations:
a colorful, eventful life.

at the end of that interview
he shared with me his understanding
of basic human psychology:
"Mr. Paul, the way I sees it is...

some peoples is wrapped too tight...
and other peoples ain't wrapped too tight...'

11

MINDS LOST

Crumbling is not an instant's Act
A fundamental pause
Dilapidation's processes
Are organized Decays —
> Emily Dickinson

by now,
I've seen
quite a few
people
lose
their minds.

have also
known
a bunch
more folk
with only
a passing
relationship
to everyday
sanity.

vividly remember
aunt Catherine
kicking aunt Elenore
at grandpa's wake
when I was twelve.
people scampered
to separate them.
calm the wild
woman down.

or when Mrs. Iffolesse
threw all that shit
out the second floor
window on 62nd
street around
the corner.

or that poet dude
in college
who could
only sit
and stare
out at
the horizon
after all
that acid.

just walking round
New York City
in my late
teens and early
twenties

was often a visit
to the coo-coo's nest:

once I passed
an emaciated woman
clad only in a mask,
panties,
and two Dixie cups
on the upper west side.
I asked a cop
what we could do.
 "wait." he said.
soon she'll walk
out of my precinct."

my mom had a sister
who spent almost
her entire adult life
in the state mental
hospital.
that other sister,

Catherine.
only checked in
and out
on occasion.

breakdowns
can be brief
or permanent:
sad and lonely
horrors.
desperate fears.

centers crumbling.
dissolving worlds.

but the slow descent
of Alzheimer's can
can be excruciating.

minor lapses
grow to major gaps
forgotten dates,
names,
appointments,
threads of conversation,
story lines,
numbers,
inevitably defy
adjustments,
accommodations
reminders,
diaries, journals,
devices...

autonomy
cedes
territory
until
solitary
confinement
locks down
the soul
handcuffs it
to the mind
then

cascades
over
the edge
into the abyss
together.

12

THE RUBYFRUIT

Down low underneath
the dense bush
at the top of the crack
near the base of the trunk
was this amazing ruby red
fruit that hung soft
luscious, dark and full
and begged to be
licked ever so softly
and sucked ever so gently
till swelling juices made
the membranes stretch
and the berry sag,
pout and pucker...
begging to be pricked
softly.

13

FOREHIMPLAY

she grabs
his purple knob firmly.
with a knowing grip.
round the shaft, down.
then pulling the loose skin
gently up. Reaches
underneath to greet his
saggy sac, which tightens
as the rod begins to swell
against the warmth of her
hands, thickening.
(blood throbbing pause)

she pumps the action,
loading the shotgun,
and the head pulses full
red and shiny.

she looks down and smiles,
eyes twinkling
teeth glimmering
just before

her head falls
(cascading hair)
and her mouth
gorges on his
bloodrushed
bone.

14

I WAS IN LOVE WITH A MEMORY THAT FELT LIKE YOU

swaddled
in your arms
breast pillowing
onto my face
mouth
gasping
flesh

my greedy tongue
remembers
ancient love ...
primitive.
raw.

needy satisfaction
nestled
in comfort
luxuriating

in undivided
gaze.

the infant nurses.

15

OUR SMORGASBORD

Our loaves stacked
against each other
crusty outsides
piping hot soft centers
on the broad table
full of party feast dishes:
your rump roast
my shank of lamb
with baby reds
your meat balls
my sausage
our saucy
tagliatelle

and paella
and osso buco
and nasi goreng

and poached pears
crème brûlée
lychees in sweet syrup
flan

and deep
dark coffee
with heavy cream

16

SEPTEMBER

each September
rewinds
the montage
of nightmare
silent clips
replaying
horrific
scenes:

aircraft gliding
soundlessly
into concrete
catastrophe.

the damned
in the infernos:

the jumpers
sailing past
hitting
the streets;
the firemen

climbing scaffolds
to their executions

the towers
endlessly falling
avalanches of
steel, glass,
and concrete.
I turn
startled
to face
the rushing
cacophony,
enveloped
in a crimson
cloud of hellish flash
vaporizing
my screaming thoughts
in an excruciating instant.

I'm hurrying down
crowded dark
smoky stairs
on muscle
cramped legs
a deafening
roar of fiery ruin
descending from above
quieting the roar.
I'm huddled
in the back
of a plane
knowing but

frozen. numb,
in paralytic fright...
colliding headlong into
red and white noise and
incinerating heat.

I'm leaping
my shirt billowing
in the roaring wind
the sun singeing
my already seared neck
dropping in blind panic
down past
swift stories
before I fly
into the shadows;
smash into the pavement.
I'm saying good-bye to my wife
on a stranger's cell phone.
I'm so sorry
that I can't think of
anything to say
other than I'm so sorry
then I mumble something
I cannot
hear above the chaos
that engulfs me.
I'm shivering
in safety
after running
shamelessly
for my life
quivering

in self-loathing
for not saving
somebody
anybody...
I'm carrying a very
heavy black lady
a very long
way to find
she's already dead
when we reach shelter...

each September still
rewinds and replays...

17

AFTERLIFE*

She pulled her panties up over those lovely
olive thighs shrouding one last time the wry
caesarian grin above her dense bush.
Tucked the bag of cash down deep between
her legs and camouflaged it all with baggy
pants and a long woolen sweater. Her savings
banked below, she pocketed two large bills
to bribe her way past peril.

"Heaven is divine nothingness," my Bosnian beauty
smirked, touching my cheek, standing before me.
*"We have the chronicle of Sarajevo to remind us
not to reach beyond ourselves."* she murmured.

Nothing I could do or say to stop her. We were both
so sick of the monotony laced with random atrocities...
Pigeons pecking through minefield rubble.

Finally, I let her pull herself away.

Watched her down the stairwell. She did not look back.

Not even as she climbed aboard the bus.
I fogged the window with sobs as the coach departed,
diesel fumes clouding the street. Kissed the cool pane
with chapped lips. It was a corpse.

Clawed my way up to a secluded sniper's perch.
Followed the route with a rifle scope through the
city to the checkpoint. Watched them stop the vehicle;
lead the passengers off. But then they stood beyond
my sights for an eternity. Heard delayed reports
following wisps of smoke.

When the bus left I could make out two rag dolls
carelessly tossed into a ditch. One leg awry.
"Are those her trousers? Is that her shoe?"

A black leathered Serb stood on the roadway,
bold as a swollen cock. One hand held
an AK 47. The other clenched something small.

I pulled the trigger and watched him drop.

* With homage to Mario Susko's Beyond.

18

MONTAGE

The dog awakening from his dream without his imaginary bone becomes the little boy holding an empty cone with the scoop lying between his feet becomes the family arriving for the fireworks just after the finale becomes the patient customer who waited interminably on line for the now sold out item becomes the breathless passenger watching his plane take off becomes the child walking the hot summer's streets with nobody out to play with becomes the diner told by the waitress that the last special has just been served to the person at the next table becomes the writer whose article is completely lost when his computer crashes becomes the fly smashing against the window pane instead of soaring freely out there becomes the base runner picked off at second becomes the jump shooter stuffed in mid-air becomes the runner stopped at the goal line becomes the race horse nipped at the finish becomes the woman distracted just before climax becomes the commuter who runs to catch the subway as the door closes in his face becomes the mosquito smashed just before digging into flesh becomes the picnicker biting down on the luscious burger as it slips out of the bun into the dirt becomes the couple just about to passionately get it on when the child bursts crying into the room becomes the guys stuck in traffic as the big game begins becomes the newly infatuated twenty-something waiting vainly for last night's hook-up to call becomes the guy in the short line watching the people in the long line move past him to their check out becomes the travelers seeing their exit as they flash by it on the interstate becomes the woman with the shard of glass in her foot sitting endlessly in the emergency room becomes the host realizing that the main course has just burned in the oven as he was fiddling with his guest's flowers becomes the golfer just rimming the cup for the par putt becomes the gardener discovering her tomatoes devoured by the groundhog becomes the parent investigating her quiet toddler to find scribbling on the white wall ...

19

HOME THEATER OF SOAP OPERATICS

A Villanelle:

at home we improvise our play
and stage the house with set designs:
the drama unfolds a bit each day,

as we script out what to say,
we block the action, run the lines,
at home we improvise our play.

The dialogue rambles, drifts astray.
The plot meanders, twists, entwines...
the drama unfolds a bit each day.

Some discourse boring and cliché
some malicious, some benign
at home we improvise our play

We throw a brickbat or bouquet,
we laugh, we cry, we moan, we whine,

the drama unfolds a bit each day

a jumble of intrigues all the way
from ridiculous to the sublime
at home we improvise our play
the drama unfolds a bit each day.

20

LEGACY: REMEMBERING RUDY (1915-2012)

First of all, I must be clear. I loved my father. And, I respected him. I admired his incredible self-discipline, his physical strength, his dogged determination, his generosity, his craft, and his artistry. I loved his gentle wit and warm humor, his loyalty to my mother, and his sweet regard for his grandchildren. I always thought of him as a man of solid principles, consistent honesty, and unfailing dependability.

These good feelings for him were, by and large, constants throughout my life. But. Truth be told, he was also, from time to time, the single most confounding and challenging person I have encountered in my entire existence. And I've met some pretty tough cookies in my line of work. Of course, I didn't have to live with or under or down any of the others.

At different times in my life, I also feared, and resented my father, and hated how my dad left me feeling. Sometimes I would be furious at him. Sometimes truly embarrassed by and for him. In the end, I found more patience, acceptance, and compassion for my dad. Even a touch of pity, which, would have, when he was younger, really ticked him off. But near the end he was grateful for any recognition or understanding of his hardscrabble struggle to emerge from his immigrant, Hoboken, Depression Era, early life to provide his thrifty wife with the means to build a small but stable family from so very little.

In the very end, he became a softer, more grateful man. Befuddled at the meaning of his longevity. Vaguely proud. Vaguely impressed. Sometimes humiliated by the loss of control over his body's processes. Increasingly able to accept help he would have never been able to even picture himself receiving in the past.

Throughout much of his life, my father was a difficult person. Apparently, as a boy he was a strong willed, picky eater, with preternatural energy and a burning restlessness that set him at odds with most of his family. Near her death, his mother, Sophie Bukovec, told me that my dad was always a pain in her heart. Near his death, Rudy told me that neither of his parents ever thought he'd amount to much.

It is a testimonial to his life that he amounted to quite a bit. Rudy was a highly skilled craftsman. He decorated cakes with some of the finest artisans in New York City. Rudy was practically swami-like in his mastery of Hatha Yoga. He stood on his head well into his 90's.

Rudy was always the hardest working man in any shop he worked in. And, quite possibly any room he stood in. He could have exhausted the energizer bunny.

This eighth grade educated man read Aldous Huxley and Edgar Casey assiduously. He studied the stock market and invested mostly quite wisely. He was a devout Roman Catholic, but was an ecumenical acceptor of any strongly held religious faith.

People recognized him as a man of strength and integrity and fine posture. He was a natty dresser till he decided not to bother nearer the end. Well- mannered with his own version of working-class polite, he was viewed with respect in the neighborhood. Unfortunately, this attribute sometimes led my mother to call him a "street angel and a house devil".

Quite moody, given to bitter and angry outbursts, he could be domineering, opinionated, stubborn, harsh, insensitive, frequently un-empathic, occasionally purposefully unfriendly, and usually extremely difficult to work with. His pessimism and negativity grew incrementally with age. He was an oft times pretty gloomy guy till his last couple of years. And for most of those final months and days he was medicated.

He often seemed happiest working alone in a perpetually-in-motion swirl of hyper focused activity. Though generally somewhat misanthropic, he had a short list of people he had greatly admired throughout his life. The longer he lived the clearer it became that most of those people were already dead.

His favorite subjects were generally things he felt passionately pissed off about: the government, processed food, the medical establishment, and the devolving state of the world. He would also hold forth, at the drop of the hat, about Yoga, healthy eating, and the magical "food value" of things like garlic or cider vinegar. Chances were, he'd cover most of those topics in one rant regardless of which one he had begun with. He didn't seem to notice the other person's eyes glazing over or their suppressed yawns.

To be fair, a lot of people found my father quite interesting... At least for a while. And sort of charmingly eccentric... at least for a while... He actually knew a lot about Yoga and health food and baking and cooking and cars and other stuff. But after a while, his sheer relentlessness and abrupt shifts of focus, and the fact that he had set up his beach-head from which to launch his next barrage right up under your nose eventually wore many folks down.

My father was also a hand cruncher: He was one of those men who while shaking hands with other men, insist on making a rather painfully strong impression. Earlier in his life, perhaps it was to make it clear that he was way stronger than he looked. He was. Later in his life, perhaps it was to show that he was still very powerful. He was.

And somewhere along the line he also began to incant a little formulaic aphorism while he grabbed the other person's **second** hand as well: "from my strength to yours and from your strength back to mine" A nice sentiment perhaps, but most guys just showed a look of pained befuddlement as they were having their **both** hands crushed by a little old wild-eyed wiry guy. I looked away whenever I could.

It's more amusing in retrospect. In real life and real time, it was quite a jumble of feelings and memories and complex twisted reactions.

My dad had incredibly strong hands because he worked hard with them from a very early age. He started helping out in his own father's bakery at the age of eight. Those hands worked thousands and thousands of pounds of bread and cake dough. Made a million rolls and pastries and cookies and cakes. Chipped and caulked the hulls of war ships in the shipyard. Built truck bodies for Adam Black. Worked on family cars at all hours. Dug gardens and cleaned a myriad of things.

They were incredible hands. Big wide palms and broad thick fingers. Usually there was a recent cut or gauge whose healing was delayed by the constant motion those hands were involved in. Permanently calloused, weathered, surprisingly deft, my father's hands could handle seriously hot objects.

He had proud working-class hands. They were not catching or throwing hands. They were not playful hands. They were not caressing hands. They were working hands attached to strong arms that also bore many scars of oven burns and the nicks and cuts from reaching in and under and around so many projects.

And his shoulders were broad, and his ribcage formed the slats to a moderate sized barrel chest. But he was, surprisingly, not a big man. He was, in fact a welterweight who came on like a light heavy.

Back in the old neighborhood growing up in North Jersey my friends thought my dad looked like Cheyenne Body, a TV western character played by a 6" 6" actor. Rudy was 5' 7" at his tallest. But he stood ramrod straight, and carried himself with a large presence. And we were rather short at the time.

Rudy's presence was awe-inspiring for me as a boy. It was also sometimes startling and scary. He would come home from working 10 or 12 hours in the bakery, tired and hungry, slightly pumped up from taking two steps at a time, up eight flights of stairs, to our fourth-floor apartment. He'd burst through the door like John Wayne arriving to deal with whatever situation needed fixing. If my sister and I were messing up or fooling around too much, he might strike swiftly and hard.

Once in his early eighties as we walked on a Jersey beach, he uncharacteristically reflected back on his parenting skills and said cryptically: "We were so young, we didn't know much..." Which I took as a sort of kind of apology. And have cherished it ever since...

Rudy was a jumble of paradoxes. An incredible driver with excellent judgment and an exquisite feel for the machines he piloted over the years, he, nevertheless, had a very terrible sense of direction. Throughout my childhood I was led to believe that Perth Amboy was at least four hours from West New York. On a good day.

He was an archetypical embodiment of the kind of ethnic clannishness and defensive xenophobia that is often found in immigrant families. BUT, while he could sometimes sound like Archie Bunker, he was just as able (and likely) to cite and enjoy as many positive attributes of most nationalities as he was able to stereotype and disparage them. And very late in his life under the softening influence of medication, he was even able to do this for the Germans.

He was vigilantly suspicious and expectant of the worst in human nature like many greenhorn kids. He had almost no use whatsoever for organized charity. Except for the Salvation Army and the Alliance of Christians and Jews. And he was an extremely generous man. Shirt off his back generous. Unless you asked for it. Then it definitely depended on the mood he was in. And that was totally a crapshoot.

In his early nineties, he lived with Gloria and me for about ten months. Felt like years. Seemed usually to have a dense storm cloud over his head. And a chilly wind in his face. He complained about most everything.

But my fondest recollection from that period was dancing around each other in the kitchen where we took sweet pains to maneuver back and forth each other and kept out of each other's way as he baked and I cooked... And he actually admired my work with food and kept his promise not to tell me how much flame to use under my pots.

He went back on his own to an apartment from there. That lasted another eight-ten-months till he wound up with congestive heart failure, a pacemaker and residence in an assisted living home.

Rudy was always the crooked hair: the one that formed his own solitary one strand cowlick: thick and coarse, stubborn and resistant and usually bending in an opposite direction.

In the assisted living facility, he found himself on a very sparsely populated head with other crooked hairs, all twisted there and here, not touching or joining any part or wave or comb-over. And even there he was malcontented. Till a couple of medical emergencies delivered him to skilled nursing care: a terminal sentence as it turned out. But also a kind of blessing in disguise.

In skilled nursing, he grew more mellow. Possibly influenced by psychiatric medications he would have eschewed with virtually all other "chemicals" for the previous 95 years. Possibly also because this otherwise proud and blue collared independent man had to finally accept the weakening of the body he had so carefully maintained throughout his lifetime. His newfound mellowness was quite a gift to the few of us that survive him and knew him over time.

It was a satisfaction and a relief to see him finally at a greater ease. To see him at last with a mind finally at peace in the body he no longer mastered. A reversal of the struggle of Rudy's entire life.

He sat and then laid peacefully concaving inward, slowly loosening the ties to the present, connecting to mostly pleasant memories in the past and mooring himself gratefully in a quiet peace as the end came...

And I am grateful to have known him this way. And to have been raised by such an unusual, eccentric, complex and yes, confounding human being who showed and taught me so much about how and how not to be in this tough life...

A close friend wrote to me this week that Rudy "lived in a ferocious fire and the embers burned on for such a long time". I love this way of expressing how Rudy was and how the fire gradually, very gradually burned down.

And as the coals persisted in the cooling ash, Rudy told me several times that he was learning an important new something. He told me was learning "acceptance". I hope to continue to learn from his example...

21

SUNDOWNING: NIGHT VIGIL

We watch the baseball game with the sound off,
neither of us into it, but not really knowing
what else to do to wind down the arduous day of
hospice nurses, vital signs, fitful sleep and a

terrible weakness that had made it impossible
for dad to even sit up in bed. As soon as I shut
off the set, a fierce fire ignites behind his now
wild eyes and he sets off on a non-stop ramble:

*His mother never liked him. His father never thought
he'd amount to much... how he had to prove himself
the hardest working man in every bakery shop...*
the Ativan slipped under his tongue doing absolutely

nothing to even slow the onslaught. I beg him to
close his eyes and fall asleep. Which he does. Just
long enough to let me drift off a little before he startles
me awake: ***"I HAVE TO PISS, I HAVE TO PISS!"***

"Hold on, dad, I'll get the bottle." I sit him up, lift
his legs, swing them, and yank his dead weight
to the edge of the mattress. He groans in pain.
I realize that his penis has been trapped beneath

his body as I drag him towards me. Tilt him back.
Reach under. Fish his squished johnson
out from under him, and stick it in the wide
mouthed urinal, feeling a peculiar sense of

resigned squeamishness, standing in wonder
at how it has come to this. The only other time
I'd ever even *seen* my father's penis, I was 12
years old in a locker room. Now I'm 65 and he

is 96 and I'm pulling on his dick, and feeding it
into a plastic vessel, urging him to just let go.
This is *son-is-father-to-the-man he barely recognizes*
And the reverse turns out to be even truer:

When I've disposed of the vile dark reddish fluid,
and I'm tucking him back in bed, he pierces me
with feverish eyes, looking like he's staring at
an almost total stranger. Asks me if I have

a job or a place to live, cause he could put me up,
maybe hire me to take care of him. Calmly,
wearily, I reassure him that he's just a little confused;
that we both need to rest; and that he needs

to close his eyes. Which he does. Just long enough
for me to hunker down and doze off once more...

"WHAT'S YOUR FAVORITE BEER?" "huh???...
Yuengling" I whisper groggily. *"ME TOO!"* he yells:

"Do we have any here?" *"No dad..."* I get up and
pull a champagne cork from a large Belgian Ale
I smuggled in months ago. Pour him a tiny plastic
medication cup full. He downs it in one deliberate gulp.

Beaming, he says coyly, *"Tastes like more!"*
We repeat the ritual four more times. Finally,
he says, *"I'll sleep good now."* Which he does.
But I am wide eyed throughout the very long night.
Wondering where this goes from here...

22

REMEMBERING JENNIE
(1915-2005)

Mother (rocking and hugging the little boy to her breast and snuggling him) *"How much do you love me?"*

Little boy (giggling and thrilled*) "more than all the houses and all the trees, and all the buses and all the..."*

Mother (squeezing him harder): *"HOW MUCH DO YOU LOVE ME?"*

Little boy (delighted and devoted and thinking fast): *"more than all the park benches and all the cars and all the flag poles and all the blades of grass and all the..."*

My mother, Jennie was a sweet, charming, nurturing, first generation Eastern European working-class woman. She was a fiercely loyal mother, a doting grandmother and a tragically disappointed wife. She was usually warm, engaging, witty, gracious, insecure, painfully vulnerable to criticism, generally anxious and ongoingly worried. Throughout her life she had a smoldering burn of dissatisfaction at her core that she endeavored "to make the best of."

In some ways she did. In other ways she could not.

She was earnest, and stubbornly convinced both of the sincerity of her good intentions and of the absolution that sincerity earned her for any hurt she might have caused. She rarely admitted being wrong. She was forever "making peace" without almost ever acknowledging an offense.

She also hardly ever admitted to personal flaws, defects or idiosyncrasies: She was hard of hearing for at least twenty-five years before conceding to her auditory problems. She always had a rather low pain threshold and took much longer than most folks to heal or recover from illness or injury. She took any reference to any of these characteristics as a serious personal insult.

My mother was stylish. A talented seamstress, she also had a great eye for color, cut and fabric. She dressed within her means but quite tastefully. She loved compliments on her outfits and wasn't above coy fishing expeditions to accidentally snag those compliments.

She was a great shopper, an experienced bargain hunter, a fine housekeeper, a very decent cook, a consummate telephone schmoozer, a wonderful nursemaid for sick people, excellent with numbers, a funny quipster, and a good friend to many. She was a devout Catholic and yet pretty open-minded and tolerant.

My mother was, first and foremost and always a family-oriented woman. She was housewife/ homemaker in the classic sense of the words. Her home and her children and their children were her defining reasons to be. She worked diligently to maintain her immediate family ties and to sustain connections with the extended families of origins. Holiday meals were always important ceremonies. Picture taking was a sacred ritualized process of recording yet another milestone of family togetherness.

Unfortunately for her, the family was usually not actually as close or content as the pictorial history suggested. And she, in particular, rarely seemed as happy or satisfied as those frozen moments indicated. Yet she clung to that photo album record of an idealized fantasy never quite lived.

She perpetually carried a deep-seated sadness about the relationship she had and a melancholy for the marriage she never had. Rudy, her husband, was always too moody, too difficult, and too angry for her to truly make a peace with him for extended periods of time. For many, many years she unabashedly confided in her children, even when they were quite young. about her frustrations and wounded feelings. Trapped by class, religion and culture in a union that was as much a sentence as a commitment, she reserved most of her complaints and resentments for one or two close friends and for her son and daughter. Venting to her kids about their father seemed entirely appropriate to Jennie. For decades, her own mother, Anna, had used Jennie as confidant about her hard life with Anton, the harsh patriarch. It seemed simply a natural progression of a long tradition of long- suffering mothers seeking solace. Eventually she confided in her granddaughters and daughter-in-law about Rudy as well.

Jennie made friends with women easily. She had a gift for making unthreatening contact with any woman whom she could read as mirroring back an openness or down-to-earth-ness. Safety perceived, mom could and would connect freely. She avoided people she believed to be overly sophisticated, or upper class or haughty in any way. She loved to talk about the ups and downs of every-day life. While not particularly worldly wise, she acquired quite a storehouse of knowledge about human nature and human relations. She knew a lot about people. Eventually she was truly people-wise, even as she was naïve to many of the ways of the world.

She loved to have her opinion solicited. And she didn't usually require a solicitation to offer her opinion. She was not, however, particularly pushy, especially outside her family. Mom delivered advice pretty carefully. People sought her out for her compassionate ear and soulful personal responses.

With her own children she might nudge or obliterate the boundary out of her sense of maternal entitlement. She was more cautious about these violations with her son. She grew to fear his stepping back. With her daughter she took more liberties. The tie was stronger by nature and felt necessity.

She dressed her firstborn in carefully handmade clothes. She primped and doted on her daughter until her son was born and after that trained her girl to be the helpmate understudy she had been for her own mom. Jennie was genuinely awed by the task of socializing and training her children for a world that her own parents had very imperfectly mastered as semi-literate immigrants. She was worried for her children, but especially her daughter.

Jennie took very seriously the scary responsibility of passing on the skills, mysteries, and dangers of being female. She cobbled together lore, lessons and dogma from her semi-invalid Croatian mother, her sisters, friends, and as much of the culture she could trust to borrow from: movies, soap operas, magazines, newspapers and TV. She worried for her daughter's safety in the scary world. She protected her overly. And held on tightly.

With her daughter she extended the apprenticeship as long as possible. She delighted in the mother/daughter connection, and in her girl's dependence, long after her daughter could or might have gone her own way. Jennie was a bit too thrilled to be needed and/or the authority for consultations on cooking and household problems. Too often her fine tutelage implied invidious comparisons to the right way, which was, of course, Jennie's. She may not have realized it, but Jennie really enjoyed being a hard act to follow. And, in many ways she was. Her frugality, flair, gregariousness, common sense, solid values, energy and generosity were strengths that usually overshadowed her vulnerabilities, vanities or guilt inducements.

It was hard not to feel guilty for going against her, or away from her. And there were good feelings for going with her.

My mother sure made you feel special even as she admonished you against being too proud.

Coincidentally she cherished and coddled those qualities in her son that most satisfied the needs she couldn't get fulfilled with her husband. She supported her son's expressions of sensitivity, stroked his attentiveness, indulged his humor, and encouraged his affection by rewarding him with hers. She told him he was more like her than his dad, encouraging them both to overlook the obvious ways that, in fact, he *was* like him. She supported her boy's interests: took pride in his accomplishments, encouraged his curiosities and explorations and ultimately mourned his independence and the distance he chose to try to be his own man.

She silently suffered through his first choice of a wife: someone whose sophistication, intellectuality, and aloofness seemed polar opposites to Jennie's attributes. She embraced his second choice warmly when she passed the litmus test by showing warm enthusiasm to a ceremonial review of a photo album of all of the son's early years. Jennie was grateful to find her son with somebody who was humble and down-to-earth: someone who would occasionally feel comfort and comforting under her wing; someone who welcomed her warmth.

She was a careful and generous mother-in-law, having been years ago purified by fire in that forge herself. She engaged in playful banter with her son-in-law and chatty storytelling with her daughter-in-law. She admired outfits. Wore gifts while visiting. Kept quiet about religion. Remembered preferences. Suffered silently through intrafamily feuds. Tried not to interfere. Or, at least be subtle and indirect if she did.

Jennie Bukovec lived to be 90 years. The last few were fairly rough. Dementia incrementally sapped her balance, strengths and abilities; gradually stealing most of her most valued skills like her gift for figuring, her sharp memory, and her good fashion sense dressing herself. When she first lost her capacity to keep her checkbook or do her taxes, she was confused and crestfallen. But she seemed insulted to have to consider the possibility that she had an illness or a disorder and she displayed a wounded, how-dare-you-agree-with-that-doctor-about-there-being-something-wrong-with-me reaction to her children.

She began hoarding and hiding things and forgetting utterly to where or how they had disappeared. Writing down a few thoughts on a greeting card, hitherto one of her happy chores, became a teary blanked out frustration. She mourned the loss of her signature talents and those jobs that had been hers in the division of labors in her marriage: Rudy took over in the kitchen. He also did most of the cleaning. Jennie felt more and more useless. She spent far too much time without the stimulation of friends or the structure of "her work". Much television began to trouble her. She would get impulses to go to a different room and forget not only what she wanted but where things were. She became less and less sure footed. She fell frequently.

Her decades long disparagement of her husband tripped clumsily and stumbled down awkwardly into a paranoid delusion that he had bought their house without her and had made it look like their old place. She complained of having no say so. And of the other people upstairs in her single family single floored home.

And all the while (at least until the last big decline) she was sweetly cordial, warm to her children and grandchildren, and still ever and always ready to dish some sweet gossip or some tragicomic human-interest story, or to retell a favorite standard from the Jennie Bukovec repertory of Tales from Life. But the list of available stories began to slowly shrink. The family pictures that had been a lifelong hobby served for a considerable time to re-weave together many of those loosening threads. Then the spark of recognition that fused perception and memory increasingly failed to ignite in her mind. Finally, the light went out behind her eyes leaving a blank emptiness. She would simply stare without apparently seeing in or out.

And Jennie was gracious and very sweet till almost the bitter very end. Then, after such a protracted graduated slip, her mind and body seemed to fall precipitously out of almost all contact. She lay for days with her eyes closed murmuring in her family dialect and fervently beseeching her parents and praying for things that just didn't seem forthcoming.

Jennie outlived her entire family of origin though she was originally the smallest and one of the least hardy of the six children from that large immigrant brood.

She outlived virtually all of her close friends.

She is survived by Rudy who stood by valiantly, and struggled in his uniquely determined, hard loving, hard headed way to care for her responsibly and respectfully and argue for her dignified death. She seemed grudgingly grateful and perhaps even a little peacefully accepting of him near the end.

She is survived by her two children, who she told regularly that she loved and was proud of even as she began to barely recognize them. They cherish many fond images of her long, confounding and nurturing life.

She is survived by a son-in-law and a daughter-in-law who miss her for the mostly sweet second mother she became to them.

She is survived by three grandchildren who will remember her warm hugs, doting concerns, and special nurturance.

She is survived by three great grandchildren who will undoubtedly carry many traces of her graces into the next generation. And perhaps a few of her terribly human flaws.

23

AT THE END OF THE LONG GOODBYE

he answered the door
ashen. atypically
happy to see me.
a surprising mix
of confusion
and relief in his eyes.

rushed me inside.
quickly closed the door.
"glad you're here...
your mother is on the floor.
can't get her up"

so began the final stage
of what had been
an excruciating descent.
a decade long slow
spiraling decline of memory,
connection and finally contact
with her shrinking circle

of intimates.

Jenny was lying flat
on her back. wild eyes
darting. stiff necked.
hair askew. a blanket
draped over her.
at the slightest touch
she would howl in agony.

dad, at wits end.
embarrassed by the ruckus.
overwhelmed. uncertain
needing me to reassure
him that we must
lift her to the bed
no matter what screams
might ensue. and that
we must also call for backup.

the EMTs were professional
and effective. mom was soon
diagnosed and admitted for
her final inpatient stay. a ninety
year old woman with dementia
and a UTI sentenced to
a deliriously confused, tortured
decline unto death. she went quietly.
whispering. murmuring. eyes
closed in silent Croatian
conversation with her mother.
and fervently, frantically, praying
the rosary. It was not pretty.

It was not gentle. It looked feral.
and frightened. not peaceful.
a cruel conclusion to a mean
disease for a sweet, generous, lady.

The finale for a life lived so humbly
and kindly deserved more
mercy and dignity and grace.
if life is not fair, death is even less so

MYTHIC MUSINGS

24. Apostates

Prometheus fashioned
a mud figure;
Athena breathed in life:
man stood upright
looking boldly into the heavens.

Zeus was not pleased.
Not flattered by
his image and likeness
emerging from the dirt.
Not happy the Titan had dared
sculpt into his creation
the posture of the gods.

Then Prometheus stole fire
from the King and
delivered it to man,
torching a path through
primordial darkness
sparking a blaze
forging tools, weapons,
and dominion over wild things.

Enraged, despotic Zeus
uttered a grotesque sentence
to set a dire warning for
any future overreachers.

Behold Prometheus
chained to rock
condemned to ages
of diurnal agony
as eagles each day
tear immortal flesh
which each day is renewed.
May gods and man alike
observe what befalls any
who challenge the almighty.
Unbowed and unremorseful
for remarkably original sins
and their wondrous results,
shackled to daily torment,
he endured it all: the promontory,
the raptors, the attacks, till eons
later Hercules freed his hero.

But still the temple priests
preach their dreadful sermons
at all those forced to listen:
to displease god is a terrible thing
to challenge god, an abomination.

Not all heed the deity's caution
nor the moral lessons of the clerics.
a fresh insurgence now arises:
they light their tapers from Promethean
flames to shine the way to fresh rebellions
and steal new powers from divinity.

24

A SPRINGTIME STORY

the dead winter
lingered past time:
everything desiccated,
brown and desolate.
the earth shivered
lilacs unborn,
as if all was in mourning for
the disgraced zealot,
now entombed:
the fever eyed man
who rallied for love and hope
and kingdoms to come, but had
failed utterly to even save himself,
falling savagely hard and alone.

inside the craggy hillside
in a cave sealed with a
rock he lay dead to the world,
broken and lifeless, his spirit having
followed after his retreating will to live:
a crushed, humiliated and forsaken man.

outside the garden was scorched:
shriveled, twisted:
vegetation skeletons
shuddering in the breeze,
shrunken husks of
past summer's bloom.

his death had been
a foregone
foretold conclusion.
he had surrendered to it
at every turn,
enduring devastating pain.

but the end brought him no relief.
no comfort.

instead he was submerged
into a hellish crossing
of cascading specters
and horrific flashbacks.

buffeted between underworlds,
he tossed in an angry rushing river
always capsizing
a-swirl and awash
in brackish whitewater
smashing against apparitions
jagged like boulders.
he was drowning.
forever.
choking.
sinking.

then,
all at once,
he seemed
sucked
suddenly
in a backward
violent vortex:
rushing in reverse.
pulled
into crushing
conscious
awareness
of unbearable
throbbing pain.

gasping dust,
heart pounding,
wounds throbbing,
choked awake

into new agonies:
a twilight dungeon:
a horror chamber,
nightmare and reality.

the cave air
cold against
his raw skin.
dank, and dark, but
shot through with
shafts of startling light
piercing through gaps

around the blocked
entrance.

he stood up slowly.
each move
cracking crusty
membranes.

tottering,
he stumbled
forward headlong
up against
the craggy surface
of the giant rock
and screamed
first noiseless
then roaring, then
he pushed against
the boulder
with desperate force.

the stone rumbled backward.

dust billowed,
sun glared,
his eyes welled up
with briny tears.
bowing down,
dazed and woozy
he saw the shimmering shadow
his gaunt body cast upon
the ground.

and this silhouette
proved
manifestly
he was still there:
he had
survived
to stand
in the sun again.

his shadow
began to vibrate
as if in celebration.
the ground was pierced
with blades of crocus
reaching through the humming soil,
and startled daffodils and tulips
burst forth in full shocked bloom.

and the smell of death
was smothered by
the clinging odor of
purple hyacinths.
robins and catbirds
descended.
bees and bugs of every sort
began to buzz and hum.
he raised his eyes
to see the spreading apparition:
squill and pansies
and primrose and forsythia
and grasses and budding shrubs
and flowering trees
blooming everywhere he looked.

he staggered forward
into the miraculous spring.

25

PAVLOVIAN POND FISH

feeling
familiar
sensations
reverberating
through
the
water
from
down
the
garden
path
as
each
step
of
seismic
thunder
nears,
the
goldfish
surge

up
from
scaly
remembrances
to
surface
startle
eyed
and
gape
mouthed
as
if
praying
for
a
new
miracle
of
manna
cast
upon
the
water
by
a
capricious
god

SPECIAL THANKS

Old friends are the best. I have several to thank for their invaluable assistance to me in the final stages of constructing this volume. Anne Schneller and Steve Laruccia, each of whom I have known more than sixty years, deserve credit for whatever modicum of presentability the reader may find in **End Pieces.** They were responsible for polishing what was my rough draft into a readable final copy. They patiently waded through a dyslexic minefield of typos and malapropisms to tidy up a space that may have looked rather more like a teenage boy's bedroom floor than a manuscript. Their patience, kindness and generosity were exceeded only by the speed with which they accomplished their tasks. Any errors you may still find here-in are attributable to last minute publisher upload malfunctions beyond their control. They also offered invaluable feedback on poem selections and exclusions, as well as for-matting.

For this collection, Anne and Steve were joined by another dear old buddy, Richard Courage, who applied his years of experience as an English professor and his talents as an author and scholar to this project. While now legally blind, Richard listened with trained ears and a keen critic's mind to this collection multiple times, offering sharp advice and lovingly careful consent. Several pieces are pithier and possibly even punchier due to Richard's feedback. I bow to "il miglior fabbro".

Yet another old associate deserves my appreciation for his ongoing encouragement and positive support in my evolution from a private scribbler to a published poet. Bill Van Buskirk, one more person I've known since my collegiate days, is an accomplished and award-winning poet with a pivotal role in the Philadelphia poetry scene. He's been a major actor in The Mad Poet's Society for two decades and now manages and hosts two different monthly poetry reading series in the area. Bill first introduced me to a reading group where I found a like minded gathering of writers who were supportive of my work. Bill also hectored me into my first published volume of poetry, **Crusty Bits Of Scrapple**, and has encouraged my progress and activity on the scene with invitations to be a featured reader on multiple occasions. His support and acknowledgment has encouraged me to produce more.

The final old friend who requires acknowledgment is my wife, Gloria Detweiler. A naturally patient human being, Gloria has been hard pressed during her erstwhile leisurely retirement years to put up with periods of my obsessive hermitage holed up feverishly writing and rewriting and endlessly wrestling with book building formatting programs. She's been kind and supportive and usually open to having later, more tossed-together meals from the family cook during his episodes of quasi creativity.